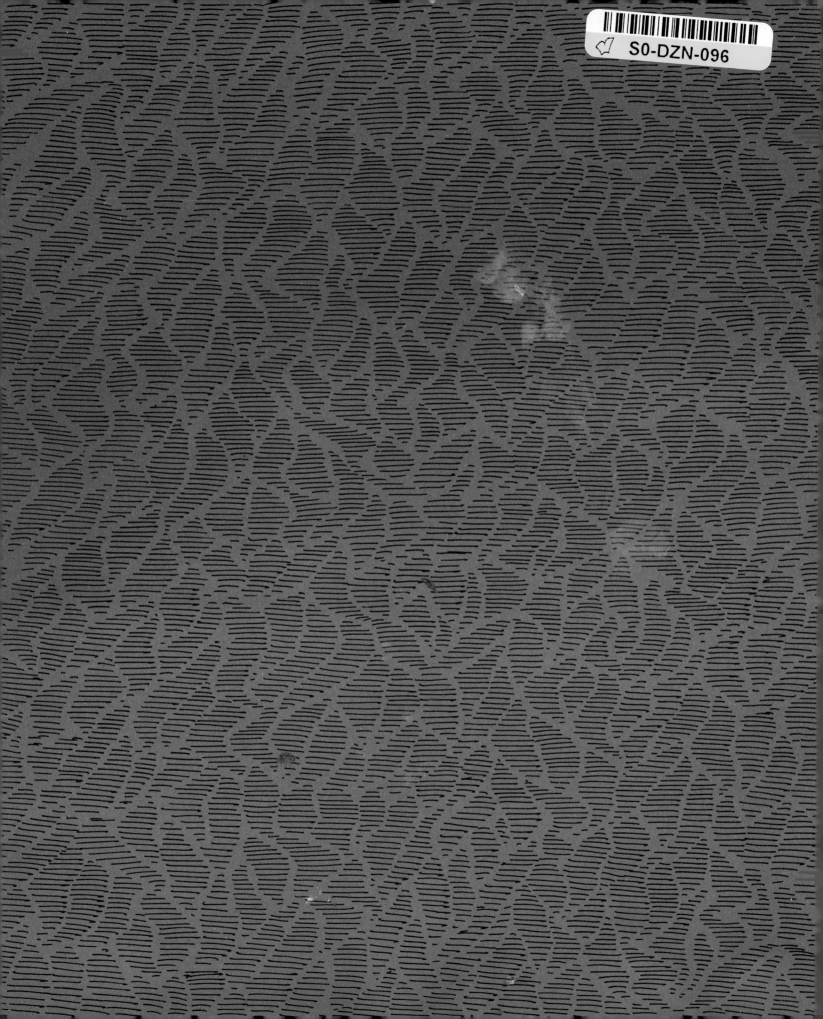

FACES IN THE DARK

A BOOK OF SCARY STORIES

KINGFISHER
Larousse Kingfisher Chambers Inc.
95 Madison Avenue
New York, New York 10016

First American edition 1994
2 4 6 8 10 9 7 5 3 1

LIBRARY OF CONGRESS CATALOGING-IN-PUBLICATION DATA
Faces in the dark : a book of scary stories / compiled by Chris Powling :
illustrated by Peter Bailey. — 1st American ed.
p.   cm.
Summary: A collection of stories about ghosts and other spooky subjects
1. Ghost stories.   2. Children's stories.   [1. Ghosts—Fiction.
2. Supernatural—Fiction.   3. Short stories.] I. Powling, Chris.   II. Bailey, Peter, ill.
PZ5.F156   1994
[Fic]—dc20 93-46911 CIP AC

ISBN 1-85697-986-5

Editor: Camilla Hallinan
Designer: Caroline Johnson
Printed in Italy

FACES IN THE DARK

A BOOK OF SCARY STORIES

Compiled by
CHRIS POWLING

Illustrated by
PETER BAILEY

Kingfisher

NEW YORK

INTRODUCTION

Some of the stories that follow are scary, some of them are strange and some may be both, depending on the kind of reader you are and where you're doing the reading. For instance, a beach in bright sunshine is probably safest—but feel free to tackle them at midnight, in the middle of winter, if you dare.

Watch out, though. All the stories were written especially for this collection except two (which are particular favorites of mine) and they'll take you right around the world—from Britain to America, from Israel to the Caribbean. So be prepared for tales that are as different from one another as a fairy story is from a campfire yarn or a news report from whispers you overhear in the playground. To appreciate their full flavor you may need to *read them aloud*. There's no better way to discover how important it is for a writer to find the right style and language for a particular subject. Mind you, before you try this you'd better make sure you haven't got a little brother or sister within earshot.

One last point. Yes, there are a few jokes on these pages, so don't worry if you want to laugh now and again. In any case, this is a perfectly normal reaction to strangeness and scariness...

Chris Powling

CONTENTS

 WIDDERSHINS
Ann Turnbull 6

 A FACE IN THE DARK
Ruskin Bond 15

 THE BRAVEST MAN IN THE WORLD
Robert Hull 18

TSIPPORAH
Adèle Geras 26

 THE ODDMENT
Chris Powling 31

 BUSH MEDICINE
Faustin Charles 38

 MINE
Anthony Masters 46

 A LOATHLY LADY
Susan Price 54

 THE GHOST ON SATURDAY NIGHT
Sid Fleischman 62

SIREN SONG
Vivien Alcock 74

WIDDERSHINS

Ann Turnbull

When they were almost there, below the granite outcrop, Mr. Ashton said they would stop and look at the view.

Michael didn't want to stop; he was eager to go on, to reach the summit. But the others were tired. Backpacks came off and hit the ground; sweaters followed.

"Can we have lunch now?"

Mr. Ashton looked at his watch; agreed. "Let's sit behind those rocks, out of the wind."

Twenty children set to with enthusiasm, unpacking backpacks, pulling out sandwiches, chocolate bars, soda cans, potato chips.

"Up there," Mr. Ashton pointed to the piled rocks on the summit, "is the Devil's Chair. See, where those rocks make a shape like a throne? They say that if you run around the Chair seven times widdershins the Devil himself will appear."

Michael stared.

"What's widdershins?" asked Paul.

"Wiggleshins, widdleshins," giggled Kelly and Zoe.

"Widdershins," said Mr. Ashton, "means counterclockwise."

Hands waved in the air, bodies turned. "That way." "No, that."

"Let's go!" Paul, Craig, and Robert were off, widdershins around the base of the rocks.

"You won't get far," called Mr. Ashton. "It's not as easy as it looks. And be careful climbing around the Chair," he added to the retreating figures of Tracey and Lorna.

"What does the Devil look like, sir?" asked Jane, a little anxiously.

"Horns and a tail," said Zoe with relish.

"Maybe." Mr. Ashton smiled. "But they say he can disguise himself. Sometimes he appears as a raven, a black dog, or a toad."

"Ugh!" said Zoe and Kelly in unison.

The class began to disperse; some went to the edge and began drawing the view; others were dutifully filling in their question sheets; the more adventurous swarmed up and around the Devil's Chair.

Michael turned widdershins.

Mr. Ashton was right. The going was hard, and it was not obvious where to go. Michael had to keep looking up at the Chair to make sure it was still on his left; but he couldn't always get close to it, and sometimes the lay of the land took him far away, and he found himself clambering over piled boulders that looked as if they had tumbled down from the summit in a storm. And it was hot; even in the wind it was hot. Only sometimes, in the lee of a rock, the wind would drop instantly, and then there was a chill, a stillness, and silence. Silence, and then, far away, it seemed, a thin piping of children, like distant birds.

He struggled on. The hardest part was just below the Chair, where the land fell away steeply in a scree. Michael slithered, and once he slid several yards, grabbing at pebbles that rolled under his hands, before he could scramble back to the safety of the big rocks.

But at last he had completed one revolution. He stepped out, dirty and bruised, and came upon sunshine, and voices, and clipboarded papers flapping in the wind, and litter-conscious Zoe chasing potato chip bags.

Michael pushed back the damp hair from his forehead. One, he thought. Six to go.

"Michael," said Mr. Ashton, "don't forget you're going to draw the view. And there's your question sheet to fill in."

Michael edged away. "I'm going around again, sir."

"Well...remind the others if you see them."

Halfway around the second time Michael caught up with Craig, Paul, and Robert, who were resting.

"Given up?" he asked.

They wouldn't admit that. "Going up to the Chair."

They tried to make it sound like a better idea than carrying on, but Michael wasn't tempted. Seven times widdershins and you'd raise the Devil. He had to make the experiment; he had to see if it

worked. Michael liked experiments. They were the only things he was enthusiastic about at school.

He went around again. And again. It was hard. His legs and shoulders ached. His hands got cut and scraped scrambling over the rocks. The boys had left the Devil's Chair but some girls were climbing on it, shouting, the wind slapping their hair across their faces.

Four times. More than halfway. He could do it. He had to do it.

Five times. Michael was exhausted. It was no easy job, raising the Devil. He wondered if it had been done before. You'd have to be desperate and believe in it.

I don't believe in it, Michael thought. And yet he needed to be sure. He couldn't let an opportunity like this pass. Test the theory. Go on. Finish.

Six times. Michael lay spread-eagled on the grass, panting. It was hot—so hot. His whole body ached. The sky glared and the rocks shimmered.

Mr. Ashton called, "Michael! We're packing up in a minute. If you want to draw your view you'd better be quick."

"Just once—once more, sir!" Michael jumped up and was away before Mr. Ashton could call him back.

But someone ran after him; a hand touched his arm. He turned. Jane.

"Don't go," she said.

Jane was small and quiet. She had never spoken to Michael before.

"Six," said Michael. "One more. I've got to."

Jane gripped his arm. "Please. Stop now."

Michael shook her off. He heard her calling after him as he struck out on the seventh lap.

It seemed quicker, easier than the others. Like the last stretch of a race, when you know you've won. He seemed to glide over the piled boulders and up and down the crags and gullies and across the scree, and suddenly he was back. He felt elated. He had done it; he had finished. Seven times widdershins—and where was the Devil?

Michael sprang down and rolled on the grass. The other children cheered. Except Jane. Michael noticed her looking up at the rocks, scared. But Mr. Ashton smiled: "Well done, Michael. Pack up your bags now, everyone. It's time to go."

They heaved up their backpacks, removed the last scraps of litter. As they turned toward the parking lot Michael glanced back at the Devil's Chair. Something moved there. Black. A dog. A big black dog bounded out from between two rocks and stood and stared at Michael.

Michael's heartbeat quickened. A raven, a toad, or a black dog.

"Michael!" Mr. Ashton called.

Michael turned. When he looked back, the dog had vanished. Stupid, he told himself. Just a dog. But where had it come from?

Back at the parking lot they saw that several more cars had appeared. Michael was reassured. The dog belonged to some visitors; it was a family pet.

They drove back to school, chattering and comparing drawings. Michael boasted about his experiment, showed off his cuts and bruises.

"Didn't see the Devil, though, did we?" said Paul.

"There was a dog—a black dog," protested Michael, and immediately felt a chill, remembering the way the dog had appeared as if from nowhere.

"I never saw it," said Paul.

But Jane had. She looked frightened.

When they arrived at school it was only half past two. Mr. Ashton said they could spend the last hour finishing their drawings or writing about the visit.

The children sighed; they were hot and restless and all they wanted was to go home.

Michael began drawing. He'd looked up at the Devil's Chair so often as he climbed around it that he thought he could draw it from memory. He drew quickly the shape of the granite throne, the tumbled rocks beneath.

When he looked at his finished picture he was pleased. It was good. But—what was that? A dark shape half hidden behind one of the boulders? Something hiding. A dog? He hadn't drawn that. Surely he hadn't. He erased it. But then he thought he saw it again, behind another rock: a muzzle, the tip of an ear. He erased vigorously and drew more rocks to hide it.

Kelly said, "Sir, there's a dog on the playground."

Michael stiffened. But the others, glad of a diversion, jumped up with a scraping of chairs and jostled at the windows as Mr. Ashton struggled to retain order.

"Sit down, Paul, Craig. Sit down, Zoe. It's just a dog. We've all seen dogs before." He paused by Michael's table. "That's coming along well, Michael."

Michael looked at his picture. What *had* he drawn? Was that a shadow behind the rocks in the foreground, or...? he scrubbed with the eraser, and made a hole.

The class settled down. Quiet returned. Coughs, rustling paper, whispers.

And then a scream from Jane. "The dog!"

Michael leaped to his feet. Chairs toppled, voices erupted. The dog—a great black hound—had reared up against the window, staring in. Mr. Ashton banged on the glass and made shooing movements. The dog dropped down, out of sight, then sprang up again; its claws scraped on the glass, scraping and scratching; saliva hung from its jaws.

Michael stood rigid with fear. Some of the children whimpered; others began banging and shooing.

"Sit down, everyone," said Mr. Ashton. "I'll get the custodian." He went out.

When he came back Zoe said, "It's gone, sir."

"Probably a stray," said Mr. Ashton. It was nearly half past three. "Pack up your things."

Michael looked at his drawing. There were no shadows now, no odd shapes, and yet . . . The picture made him uneasy. He crumpled it up and hurled it at the wastebasket. Mr. Ashton was startled. "Spoiled it," muttered Michael.

All the way home he watched for dogs. There were plenty of them, of course: terriers, German Shepherds, collies, a Great Dane stately on a leash. Once, out of the corner of his eye, he thought he saw a black dog behind a wall; then, again, padding alongside a privet hedge. He ran, banged open the gate of his front yard, beat on the front door.

"I'm not deaf," his mother said.

He was home, safe. He dumped his bag, got a drink and some potato chips, settled in front of the television.

He stayed in all evening. He ate his dinner, scribbled some homework, then went back to the television. His favorite programs washed over him, lulling and reassuring. He'd been imagining things. There were often dogs on the school

playground. And the streets were full of black dogs; it was simply that he was noticing them more today. That one behind the privet hedge, for instance: surely that was Caesar, the Wilsons' labrador? Stupid. He'd been really stupid.

He felt sleepy. The cuts on his hands smarted.

"You all right?" His mother felt his forehead.

"Tired. It was hot on the trip. We walked miles."

"You'd better get an early night."

Michael thought with unusual longing of his bedroom with its posters and comics, his Mickey Mouse alarm clock and his Batman comforter cover.

"Okay," he said.

He went slowly upstairs.

"Wash," said his mother. "Don't forget."

Michael washed briefly, leaving grubby prints on the towel. His head ached. He was sleepy, so sleepy.

He stumbled across the landing and pushed open his bedroom door.

Huge, on the bed, lay the black dog. Waiting.

A FACE IN THE DARK

Ruskin Bond

Mr. Oliver, an Anglo-Indian teacher, was returning to his school late one night, on the outskirts of the hill station of Simla. From before Kipling's time, the school had been run on English public school lines; and the boys, most of them from wealthy Indian families, wore blazers, caps, and ties. *Life* magazine, in a feature on India, had once called it the "Eton of the East." Mr. Oliver had been teaching in the school for several years.

The Simla Bazaar, with its theaters and restaurants, was about three miles from school; and Mr. Oliver, a bachelor, usually strolled into the town in the evening, returning after dark, when he would take a shortcut through the pine forest.

When there was a strong wind, the pine trees made sad, eerie sounds that kept most people to the main road. But Mr. Oliver was not a nervous or imaginative man. He carried a flashlight, and its pale gleam—the batteries were running down—moved fitfully over the narrow forest path. When its flickering light fell on the figure of a boy, who was sitting alone a rock, Mr. Oliver stopped. Boys were not supposed to be out of school after 7 P.M.; and it was now well past nine.

"What are you doing out here, boy?" asked Mr. Oliver sharply, moving closer so that he could recognize the rule breaker. But even as he approached the boy, Mr. Oliver sensed that something was wrong. The boy appeared to be crying. His head hung down, he held his face in his hands, and his body shook convulsively. It was a strange, soundless weeping, and Mr. Oliver felt distinctly uneasy.

"Well, what's the matter?" he asked, his anger giving way to concern. "What are you crying for?" The boy would not answer or look up. His body continued to be racked with silent sobbing. "Come on, boy, you shouldn't be out here at this hour. Tell me the trouble. Look up!" The boy looked up. He took his hands from his face and looked up at his teacher. The light from Mr. Oliver's flashlight fell on the boy's face—if you could call it a face.

It had no eyes, ears, nose, or mouth. It was just a round smooth head—with a school cap on top of it! And that's where the story should end. But for Mr. Oliver it did not end here.

The flashlight fell from his trembling hand. He turned and scrambled down the path, running blindly through the trees and calling for help. He was still running toward the school buildings when he saw a lantern swinging in the middle of the path. Mr. Oliver stumbled up to the watchman, gasping for breath. "What is it, Sahib?" asked the watchman. "Has there been an accident? Why are you running?"

"I saw something—something horrible—a boy weeping in the forest—and he had no face!" "No face, Sahib?" "No eyes, nose, mouth—nothing!" "Do you mean it was like this, Sahib?" asked the watchman, and raised the lamp to his own face. The watchman had no eyes, no ears, no features at all—not even an eyebrow! And that's when the wind blew the lamp out and Mr. Oliver had a heart attack.

THE BRAVEST MAN IN THE WORLD

Robert Hull

There was once a man so brave that nothing scared him, not bears, or snakes, or flying arrows, or the shouting of thunder.

Not even ghosts scared him. Outside the village one night, from down by the river, there was a whistling and hooting like owls. "Listen," an old man said, "ghost talk. The ghosts are talking about death and ghastly things, telling ghost stories." His words sent a chill down the spines of the people listening around the fire, but the young man felt only curious to see these ghosts.

He slipped away into the shadows and went toward the river, hoping to find some skeletons sprawled under a tree, chatting in that whistling way that he'd just heard.

He didn't see any ghosts, because the three who were there saw him first. They were having their evening meal, the smells of chicken and fish that drifted from the village. Ghosts don't eat; all they need to keep them alive is the aroma of food.

So when they looked along the path and saw a young man creeping toward them they slid off in their canoes, gliding through the water quicker than otters; ghost canoes have holes in them and go faster than the canoes of people. Even the brave young man might have shuddered if he'd seen three misty skeletons speeding along in holey canoes, and if he'd heard the clinky, rustling sounds of paddling bones.

After a while the three ghosts stopped and pulled their canoes up the riverbank.

"You know," one of them said, "I think I'll go and scare that young man for spoiling our meal. I'll jump out at him on the path and dance around him rattling my teeth."

"I'd like to do that, too," said the second ghost.

"I'll go," said the third ghost. "I'm the biggest, so I'll give him the biggest fright. I'll scare him silly."

"It's not how big you are," said the first ghost, "it's how scary."

"I suggest a wager," said the third. "Whoever scares that young man the most wins the others' canoes."

"How about a bigger bet? How about our horses? They can take us everywhere."

"Horses it is."

So it was arranged. The next night the first ghost paddled up to the village, to give the young man the scare of his life. He walked along the path—peddling along in the air a foot or two above ground, the way ghosts do—to the edge of the forest, where the path from the village reached the trees. He sat on a branch and started whistling a well-known tune, swinging his legs in time to the rhythm.

In no time at all the young man, as curious as the night before, came creeping across from the village, peering into the trees.

The ghost carried on whistling till the young man saw him and stopped. Then—GOOOOR, GRAAAR, RRAAAAHHR!—the ghost swung out of the tree with a howl, rattling his teeth and whirling his crackling arms around as fast as he could. Then he started jinking around and making hooting noises.

The ghost waited for the young man to turn and run. But the young man only listened, and looked for a moment, then jumped forward and grabbed an arm bone with one hand and an ankle-bone with the other. The ghost's hooting turned to a howl as the young man bent his skeleton around into a hoop, and tied it with some grass. Then he started rolling his hoop along the path. The ghost moaned and whined with every clanky revolution of the bones. "Don't, don't," it yelled.

They came to the river. The skeleton trundled in and splashed over.

"You look as if you need a good wash, ghost! Your ghost-woman will appreciate it!" And the young man laughed.

Ghosts can't

drown, of course, but this one thrashed about in the moonlit river as if it thought it could. To the young man it was a pretty sight, this ghost taking a bath of glitter. After beating about like a trapped salmon for a minute or two, the ghost finally snapped the grass knot. It staggered back upright and clinked out, dripping like a fish basket.

When the other ghosts heard what had happened, they rattled and shook with laughter so much that they had the kind of accident that sometimes happens to ghosts. They laughed their heads off. Two skulls rolled down the bank into the river. Two piles of bones skittered after them into the water, feeling around on the sandy bottom till each found a wet skull and crammed it back on. At first the big skeleton had the little one's skull on, which slipped off; the smaller skeleton went tottering around wearing the tall ghost's skull. It took a minute or two till they got sorted out with the right heads.

The next night the second ghost went to the village. When the young man came along, the ghost jumped out of hiding and threw an arm around the young man's neck, hissing, "Dance with a ghost! Swing along with a skeleton!"

"I think I'd like that!" the young man calmly said, putting his arms around the ghost. The ghost couldn't believe its ear sockets. It couldn't break free, either. The young man's hands had a tight grip on the dry bones of his partner's as they started swaying from side to side. "I'm dancing with a ghost," the young man sang. "My partner's a skeleton. But what shall we do for music and rhythm? I know, your little echoey skull."

And as calmly as if he were taking a pot from a shelf, the young man lifted the skull off the neck and put it under his arm. Then, pulling a leg bone out from under one of the knees, he began to hammer out a catchy rhythm on the skull. "Dance with me, you dumb skull, you ghastly ghostly glum skull, let me thump your drum skull, your empty little numb skull! What a haunting rhythm I'm beating on where your brain was!"

The ghost groaned. "Don't, don't, my head hurts!"

"You haven't got a head, boneful ex-person, only a hollow skull. It can't hurt. Ghosts can't feel pain."

"This ghost can. And don't whirl the rest of me around. Don't dance me so hard. I've got dizziness in every bone!"

The young man was whirling the ghost around so fast that pieces started to fly off. A finger bone flipped through the air. An ankle slid off into the bushes. Faster and faster. One, two ribs jangled down into the dust. The ghost was in pieces. The young man laughed, watching the ghost shambling and dithering about trying to reassemble itself.

The ghost howled. "I shall tell my ghost-man about your cruelty, and he will come and scare you out of your wits."

So it was a ghost-woman he had danced with! "Even better! I've danced with a ghost-woman!" the young man cried, as the ghost-woman limped off down the path, a bone or two still missing.

When the ghost told her story, only one ghost laughed, the third one. He knew how much he was going to terrify the young man and win the bet. The next night he rode off on his large skeleton horse to find the young man.

The young man was already on the path, waiting. "I and my horse have come to kill you," said the ghost in his deepest, hollowest voice, making his skeleton horse rear up over the young man.

"You cannot kill me," the young man said. "I'm a ghost in disguise, a witch ghost with false eyes, false flesh, false teeth. I'm an illusion. I can scare you to bits." And the young man moaned and howled like a pack of wolves—HAROO! HAROOZLE! FAROOZLE! He crossed his eyes and gnashed his teeth. He made piercing whistling sounds. It would have sent a herd of buffalo thundering off in terror. The ghost started to moan and shake, limbs going every way at once, like bits of scribble. Then the horse under him began trembling, too, and after a few moments of terrible shuddering, with the ribs of the horse banging like a gate, the ghost-rider toppled off with a clatter. Ghosts can't be knocked unconscious, but this one decided to rest for a while, and just sat there.

The young man was delighted. "A horse! I have a ghost-horse! Good-bye, ghost!" And taking the skeleton horse by the bridle he

leaped on its back and rode off down the path.

It was early morning in the village when some women carrying water saw a man on a ghost-horse ride out of the mist. They screamed and ran, waking everyone around. People came peering dozily out of their tepees, wondering what was going on. In the dawn mist they saw a ghost-horse with a young man on it. A dream left in our heads from the night, each one thought. They stood rubbing their eyes, waiting for the dream to fade. But it didn't. The ghost-horse with its living rider came walking slowly through the village, the young man looking around him with a great grin on his face, his skeleton horse creaking under him from the unusual load. Everyone gaped as the young man dismounted in front of his own tepee and tethered his mount.

An old man went over, the one who had heard the ghosts talking a few nights before. He wanted to touch it, to see if it really was a ghost-horse. He patted the horse on the rump bone. It rattled. He nodded his head, as if he understood something. A few other brave people came across and stood around. Soon the young man was telling his story, and soon people were believing him.

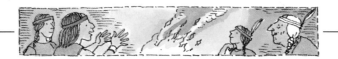

That night, around a great fire, the young man told all the people how he had put three ghosts to flight and stolen a ghost-horse. When he had told it all once, they asked him to tell it again.

"He is a very brave young man," people said to one another.

"He must be the bravest young man in the world."

"There has never been anyone so brave."

"No one will ever be able to do a braver thing than he has done."

They nodded their heads solemnly.

There were some children sitting around the fire, too. After the first hour of listening they began to get bored. A little girl, who happened to be sitting next to the young man, began playing with a piece of wood at the edge of the fire. She didn't notice when a small wood spider dropped off and ran toward the young man's foot. It ran up over his moccasin, then turned around to go down again, then decided to try further up.

The young man felt a little tickle around his ankle. He looked down. A spider!

He screamed and put his arms over his head. "Aaaaargh! Get it off me! Get it off me!" The little girl picked up the spider and put it on her hand, watching it delightedly as it scampered around her palm.

"Look! Isn't he pretty?" she said, holding it out for him to admire.

"Take it away! Take it away!" shrieked the bravest man in the world.

TSIPPORAH
Adèle Geras

Here is something I've noticed: as soon as candles are lit, as soon as night falls, my grandmother, my parents, and all my uncles and aunts start telling stories, and the stories are often frightening, meant to send small shivers up and down every bit of you. When the grown-ups talk, I listen. I never tell them *my* frightening story, even though it is true. They wouldn't believe me.

A few weeks after my eighth birthday, my grandmother took me to visit her friend Naomi. Why, I wanted to know, had I not seen this friend before?

"I never take very young children to see her. She might frighten them. The way she looks, I mean," said my grandmother.

I imagined a witch, a giantess, or some monster I couldn't quite describe. I said, "What's the matter with her?"

"Nothing's the matter with her. She's very old, that's all."

I laughed. "But you're very old and I'm not scared of you."

My grandmother said, "Compared with Naomi, I'm a rosebud, I promise you. Wait and see."

She was quite right. Naomi was ancient. Her head was like a walnut, or a prune, perhaps, with eyes and a mouth set into it. She wore a headscarf and I was glad of that. I was sure she was bald underneath it. She sat in a chair pulled up to the table, drinking black coffee and smoking horrible-smelling cigarettes. She spoke in a voice like machinery that needed oiling. After I was introduced to her, I was supposed to sit quietly while the ladies

chatted. I couldn't think of anything worse, so I said to my grandmother, "May I go out into the courtyard for a while? I'll just look at things. I promise not to leave the house."

My grandmother agreed, and I stepped out of Naomi's dark dining room into the sunshine. The rooms Naomi lived in could have been called an apartment, I suppose, but it wasn't one in a modern building. It was in a part of Jerusalem where the houses were built around a central courtyard, and four or five families shared the building. In this courtyard there were pots filled with geraniums outside one door, and some watermelon seeds drying on a brass tray outside another. A small, sand-colored cat with limp, white paws was sleeping in a patch of shade. Naomi's rooms were on the upper story of the house. It was about three o'clock in the afternoon. All the shutters were closed. Perhaps everyone who lived here was old and taking an afternoon nap. The sun pressed down on the butter-yellow flagstones of the courtyard, and the walls glittered in the heat. Suddenly I heard a noise in the middle of all the silence: a cooing, a whirring of small wings. I turned around to look, and there, almost within reach of my hand, was a white dove sitting on the balcony railing.

"How lovely!" I said to it. "You're a lovely bird then! Where have you come from?"

The bird cocked its head and looked exactly as though it were about to answer, then it changed its mind and in a blur of white feathers it flew off the railing and was gone. I leaned over to look for it in the courtyard and thought I saw it, just there, on a step. I ran down the stairs after it, but it was nowhere to be seen.

A girl of about my age was standing beside a pot of geraniums.

Where had she come from? She wore a white dress which fell almost to her ankles. I thought, She must be very religious. I knew that very devout Jews wore old-fashioned clothes.

"Have you seen a white dove?" I asked her. "It was up there a moment ago."

The girl smiled. She said, "Sometimes I dream that I'm a dove. Do you believe in dreams? I do. My name is Tsipporah, which means 'bird,' so of course I feel exactly like a bird sometimes. What do you feel like?"

I didn't know what to say. I was thinking, This girl is mad. My name is Rachel, which means "ewe lamb," but I never feel woolly or frisky. My cousin is called Arieh, which means "lion," and he's not a bit tawny or fierce. I said, "I just feel like myself."

"Then you're lucky," said Tsipporah. "Sometimes I think I will turn into a bird at any moment. In fact, look, it's happening...feathers...white feathers on my arms..."

I did look. She held out her arms and cocked her head, and I blinked in the sunlight which all at once was shining straight into my eyes and dazzling me...but in the light I could see...I think I saw, though it's hard to remember exactly, a flapping, a vibration of wings, and the krr-krr of soft dove-sounds filling every space in my head. I closed my eyes and opened them again slowly. Tsipporah had disappeared. I could see a white bird over on the other side of the courtyard, and I ran toward it calling, "Tsipporah, if it's you, come back...come back and tell me!"

The dove launched itself into the air and flew up and up and over the roof and away, and I followed it with my eyes until the speck that it was had vanished into the wide pale sky. I felt weak, dizzy with heat. I climbed slowly back to Naomi's rooms, thinking, Tsipporah must have hidden from me. She must be a child who lives in the building and likes playing tricks.

On the way home, my grandmother started telling me one of her stories. Sometimes I don't listen properly when she starts on a tale of how this person is related to that one, but she was talking about Naomi when she was young, and that was so hard to imagine that I was fascinated.

"Of course," my grandmother said, "she was never quite the same after Tsipporah died."

"Who," I asked, suddenly cold in the sunlight, "is Tsipporah?"

"Naomi's twin sister. She died of diphtheria when they were eight. A terrible tragedy. But Tsipporah was strange."

"How, strange?"

"Naomi told me stories...you would hardly believe them if I told you. I know I never did."

"Tell me," I said. "I'll believe them."

"Naomi always said her sister could turn herself into a bird just by wishing it."

"A white dove," I said. "She turned herself into a white dove and flew away."

My grandmother looked at me sharply.

"I've told you this story before, haven't I?"

"Yes," I said, even though, of course, she never had. I didn't tell her I had seen Tsipporah. I didn't want to frighten her, so I said nothing about it.

Now, every time I see a white dove, I wonder if it's her, Tsipporah, or perhaps some other girl who stretched her wings out one day, looking for the sky.

THE ODDMENT
Chris Powling

At first, I wasn't afraid of the Oddment at all. I loved everything about it—its ragged shape, its softness and smell, its colors all faded in the sun.

Where had it come from? Was it cut from an old bathrobe of my mother's? Or from one of Grandpa's ancient flannel shirts? "Never you mind," Mum always said when I asked her. "Just think yourself lucky you've got it at all."

"I do, Mum," I answered.

And I did, too.

To tell you the truth, I couldn't imagine life without the Oddment. It was my Best Friend and my Favorite Toy and my Big Brother all rolled into one. "Honestly," Mum would say, "sometimes I can't tell where that Oddment ends and you begin!"

I couldn't tell, either. That's the way it was and that's the way it always would be.

"Make up, make up,
Never, never break up . . ."

And we never would.

Not ever.

Even when I started school it made no difference. I simply took the Oddment along with me. "No problem," the teacher told my mum. "Cuddlies are welcome here."

"*Not* a Cuddly," I frowned.

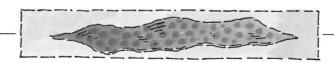

"Well, a Comforter..." said the teacher.

"*Not* a Comforter."

"A Special Thing, maybe?"

"*Not* a Special Thing," I insisted, stamping my foot. "It's an Oddment."

"It certainly is," the teacher laughed. "But whatever you call it, I wouldn't dream of telling you to leave it at home."

So all through the Infants, the Oddment and I were closer than ever.

Don't ask me why things began to change when I went up to the Juniors. At first, I suppose, I simply forgot the Oddment—and rushed back up to my bedroom at the end of the day to cover it with kisses. Then, every so often, I decided it was too much trouble to look after it amid all the hustle and bustle of the classroom. "It'll get lost," I complained. "I won't know where to find it."

"Fine," said Mum. "It's your choice."

And she winked at Grandpa as if she'd expected something like this now that I was older.

Of course, this got me so ashamed that for a while I made more of a fuss over the Oddment than ever.

But only for a while.

Soon I was "forgetting" it regularly. Worse still, when other kids came to play I was careful to tuck it under my pillow out of sight. Once, just to show who was boss, I left it in the bathroom overnight—a wet, thundery night when normally I'd have lain in bed sucking one corner of it so I wouldn't feel frightened. I slept surprisingly well...till I woke up at dawn and found the Oddment wrapped around my neck like a scarf and one corner of it actually in my mouth waiting to be sucked.

No, Mum or Grandpa hadn't put it there. I could tell that from how nice they were about it—as if they would have brought it to me from the bathroom if they'd only noticed. "You don't have to grow up all at once," said Grandpa with a grin. "Bit by bit is fine with us."

"Probably you fetched it yourself," Mum agreed. "But you were too sleepy to remember."

"Or you were sleepwalking," Grandpa added.

Mum told him off about that in case he'd scared me.

But it wasn't Grandpa who scared me. I knew exactly who'd done the walking while I was asleep.

After that, I admit, I tested the Oddment out. Each evening I stuffed it under the sofa downstairs, or hung it on the clothesline on the patio, or locked it in the tool shed at the back of the garden. But the instant I opened my eyes next morning, it was snuggled up beside me in bed.

It had other tricks, too. One of them was hiding in my lunch box so it was the first thing I saw when I lifted the lid in the Dining Hall. Another was wrapping itself around my PE stuff—or tucking itself so carefully in the back pocket of my jeans I had no idea it was there, flapping behind me like a tail, till the other kids pointed it out. "Don't worry," they always said. "We've got Cuddlies, too!"

"You have?"

"Certainly we have..."

And they meant it, I'm sure.

By now, though, I was pretty certain that their Cuddlies were nothing like mine. My Cuddly, my Comforter, my Special Thing was a complete freak. What I'd got really was an Oddment. And I was beginning to wonder if I'd ever be rid of it.

So I decided it must have an accident—an accident-on-purpose, you understand. After all, nothing could actually *hurt* an Oddment. A bonfire would simply burn it up, I reckoned, or a toilet could just flush it away under the house...

Probably you can guess what happened. Or didn't happen, rather. After this, whenever my eyes fluttered open in the morning, I found myself sucking something that was thin and frayed with a scorched, smoky taste to it and a faint smell of...well, a toilet.

No, don't laugh.

I didn't laugh, I promise you—especially now that the Oddment was so shriveled and so gristly-looking it reminded me of a stringy piece of meat, the kind

you can't swallow however hard you chew. It didn't feel like a scarf around my neck any more either... more like a strip of burlap or an old, old bandage.

By now I was desperate, I don't mind telling you. What really scared me was the thought that the Oddment might figure out what was going on—not carelessness on my part at all, but a plot to destroy it altogether. What would it do then?

Knowing Mum and Grandpa wouldn't believe me however hard I tried to convince them, I told my teacher instead. Not straight out, naturally, in case she thought I'd gone crazy, too. Instead, I wrote her a story about an indestructible Cuddly called a Whatsit—the best story I've ever written. And there, in her comments at the bottom of the page, she gave me the answer to my problem:

This is brilliant—*even from a great storyteller like you. It's so spooky it gave me a nightmare last night! Why did you leave it unfinished, though? Couldn't the Whatsit have been mailed to the other side of the world, for example—so far away it could never have hoped to get back? It isn't really fair to keep your reader guessing...*

Thanks, Miss Johnson.

I couldn't wait to get home that day.

Take my word for it, the package I bundled together was *safe*. Outside it looked like an ordinary envelope but inside was heavy-duty plastic surrounding an old tin pencil box of

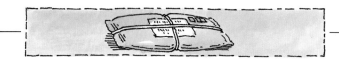

Grandpa's which I'd wrapped up tight with industrial-strength tape. A rattlesnake couldn't have broken out of that, never mind the Oddment.

Then came the real craftiness. The address I wrote on the label was to a town deep in the outback of Australia. And it was *nearly* correct...except for the person's name and house number and street. These I completely made up.

Finally, a stroke of genius, I gave the package to an uncle of mine to mail for me in America. "My friend wants a U.S.A. postmark for his collection," I explained.

Now there was no chance at all the package would be tracked back to me. It would be stored away forever in some isolated post office Down Under...

That was three years ago. In all the time since, Mum and Grandpa have mentioned the Oddment only twice. The first was one Christmas when we had a really good laugh about it. The second was last month, on my birthday, after Grandpa gave me his present—a yappy, roly-poly puppy called Spike. "Here you are, already 11 years old," he declared, "and you've never had a pet to look after—not counting that old rag you used to tote about with you, anyway. What was its name?"

"The Oddment," I said. "Spike will be much more fun than that, Grandpa!"

He certainly is. For instance, I get a present each day now. Usually it's a dog biscuit or a mouthful of newspaper or a place mat stolen from the kitchen. Whatever it is, Spike lays it on my bed as if it were some kind of treasure, then wags his tail frantically to persuade me I should take him for a walk as a reward.

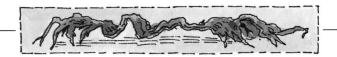

Today, though, after breakfast, he brought in something really weird from the garden. It was twisted and crusty and somehow travel-weary, like a piece of rigging from an old-fashioned sailing ship. But worst of all was its color, which reminded me of the sort of bruise Mum calls "angry."

Of course, I recognized it at once, and my heart nearly stopped in mid-beat.

There it is behind me, coiled up on my pillow, as I type all this on my computer. I've been here at the keyboard all day, to be honest. The trouble is, though I think Miss Johnson is right about how unfair it is to leave the reader guessing, I've got no more idea about the end of my story than I had the first time I wrote it. And already it's getting close to bedtime.

BUSH MEDICINE

Faustin Charles

Milton Codrington was a bachelor. He lived in a one-roomed house in St. Victoria village, Barbados. He was a poor, simple man, who didn't have a job nor a trade.

One night he had a dream that was to change his whole life. In his dream, Milton saw an old woman picking pawpaw leaves, putting them into a boiling pot, stirring the brew and saying, "Boil for a hour, wait till it cool, then drink, good for all kinda sickness."

The dream ended, Milton turned, opened his eyes, sat up in bed, then he muttered, "Pawpaw leaf. I never realize ordinary pawpaw leaf so good for medicine."

So Milton went to a pawpaw tree in the backyard of his house, picked

some leaves, boiled them in a pan for an hour, then he said, "Now, how I going to know whether this brew work or not, I not sick with nothing?"

Just then a neighbor, Ma Gerty, called to him. "Milton, boy, me granddaughter sick bad bad with the flu, and I don't know what to do!"

Milton poured some of the pawpaw leaf brew into a cup and gave it to Ma Gerty, and said, "It's like bush tea, but don't put no sugar in it, just give it to you granddaughter to drink."

Ma Gerty stared at the dark-green liquid, nodded, and said, "Boy, I ain't have much faith in these bush medicine, but I going give this to she, and thank you." And she went and gave it to her granddaughter.

About fifteen minutes later, Ma Gerty shouted from her house, "Milton, boy! It work! The girl better. Praise the Lord!" Ma Gerty was laughing and kissing her granddaughter who was sitting up in bed, smiling.

"Yes, praise the Lord!" Milton grinned. "I tell you it woulda make she better!"

Soon Milton was giving the pawpaw bush medicine to the

whole village. Then people started coming to him from all over the island. Whenever anyone became ill, instead of first going to the doctor or the hospital, they went to Milton for his pawpaw leaf brew, and they were cured of all their illnesses. Milton was convinced that the pawpaw leaf brew was a magic cure and he told no one about how he came by it. He felt that he was specially chosen by God to have the knowledge about the pawpaw leaf medicine.

Milton's fame as the man with the magic cure spread to other islands. He was a vain man, and loved the respect he was getting from all quarters. He took no money for his brew. People gave him food and clothes, that was all he would accept.

Ma Gerty always stood on the veranda of her house watching all the goings-on.

One day, when most of the people had gone away from Milton's house, two men from the city of Bridgetown came to see him. One was called Riley, who owned a dry goods store, and the other, Franklyn, a pharmacist.

"Now what can I do for all you?" Milton asked.

"Well, it's like this, Mr. Codrington," answered Riley. "We hear about you bush medicine, and we was wondering if you interested in going into business."

"Business like what?" Milton asked.

"What we mean is this," Franklyn said calmly. "You bush

medicine is popular all over the islands. Now suppose you make it and we bottle it and market it and sell it. We can make a lotta money, the three of we together.''

Milton looked bewildered.

"You can have big, big house, car and servants, and plenty other nice things," said Franklyn.

"Money mean power you know, " said Riley.

Milton smiled a little. "I always thought that bush medicine is free for all," he said. "After all, bush growing wild all over the place. People pick it and try it, if it work then they use it and tell others about it. They does never charge money for it."

"I know I was wasting me time coming here, yes," Riley raged. "The man making sport, man. It's people like you who does end up begging by the roadside, and when people check back at you life, they discover that you had a chance of becoming rich and you didn't take it."

"Riley, man, I tell you don't get on so," Franklyn pleaded.

"How you want me to get on!" Riley snapped. "The man must be crazy, that's all."

"That's not the way to talk to

people, man,'' said Franklyn who was becoming fed up with the whole idea. ''You must control youself.''

''All right, all right, man, I sorry,'' Riley said coolly.

Milton wiped his face with a dingy piece of red cloth, and studied the two men carefully. Then he said, ''All right, I go do it with all you.''

Riley laughed and said, ''Now you talking sense, man.''

''You see when you give people time to make up they mind, everything does work out all right,'' Franklyn smiled.

''Now, you must stop giving away the brew free to people, you hear,'' said Riley. ''When they come and ask you for it you must tell them, All freeness done.''

''All right, then,'' Milton nodded. ''It going to be hard, but I go stop giving it away.''

''Mr. Codrington, that'll be in the contract,'' said Franklyn, still smiling.

Milton felt a very strange feeling welling up in his stomach.

Milton went into business with Riley and Franklyn, and the business prospered. He now lived in a beautiful house with an extra large kitchen where he boiled the pawpaw leaf brew in large pots on an electric stove. He installed a telephone, and when the brew was ready he called Riley or Franklyn and they sent a van to pick it up.

They checked it, bottled and labeled it, and sold it. The profits from the business were split equally three ways.

Milton stopped giving the brew away to people who called at his home begging for it. He lied and said that he no longer made the brew, or he had forgotten how to make it.

One morning, Ma Gerty called at his home. Milton looked out of a window and greeted her sheepishly. "Good morning, Ma. How life treating you these days?"

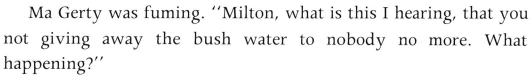

Ma Gerty was fuming. "Milton, what is this I hearing, that you not giving away the bush water to nobody no more. What happening?"

Milton tried to smile, but failed. "Ma, I stop making that. I ain't have no time with it. I doing big business with other things now."

"The other day, a woman come to you for some of the bush water and you tell she, no, you don't make it no more," Ma Gerty said. "That woman did want the medicine for she sick baby, she didn't get it, and now she child dead. You know about that?"

Milton felt sick, and he began to shake all over. "Well, I sorry about that," he said timidly, "but as I say, I ain't making the bush brew no more, it's too much headache and worry, man."

"And what about them two fellas I see that come to see you some time ago?" Ma Gerty went on. "I know that one of them is a pharmacist, and the other one own a store."

"Them is just me longtime friend, man," Milton gasped as his head ached. "I use to know them from me school days, and they did drop in to say howdy, that's all."

43

"Milton, I feel you up to something. I hope you know what you doing. You suddenly get rich overnight, you think people don't suspect you up to something, and something that not nice? You should have a little conscience, man; that woman child spirit going to haunt you."

"I don't know what you talking about, Ma, I does live a good life."

"Boy, you does get me so vex sometimes. All right, when bad luck start blighting you, don't come for my help, you hear!" Ma Gerty glared at him and went off.

And almost at once the bad luck did begin to blight.

As the days passed, Milton started to change. His fingers and arms began to look like the leaves and stems of a pawpaw tree. His hair grew long and disheveled, and his body resembled the trunk of the tree. On the soles of his feet grew tiny roots. His whole body throbbed with a burning pain, and his color changed from dark brown to green. He was ashamed and afraid to go outside his house in the daytime. He drank large quantities of the pawpaw leaf brew, hoping to get better and change back to his normal self, but the more he drank, the worse he became.

One night, when Milton was out picking the pawpaw leaves, he felt a great pain in his stomach, he couldn't move from where he was standing, and suddenly he was a pawpaw tree.

The spirit of the dead child entered the tree and it swayed in a gentle breeze...

MINE
Anthony Masters

On the wind, Jo heard someone call her name. She got off her mountain bike and listened. For a while she could hear only a curlew call. The bracken rustled, the ugly sheets of tin fencing around the old mine shaft rattled and a light plane buzzed like a mosquito in the Indian summer sky. White clouds raced above her and the moor smelled sweet.

"Jo."

She started. The call was quite clear now and there was an urgency to it.

"Jo."

She laid her bike down on the worn track and walked across to the old mine shaft that had been securely closed off years ago—though a couple of the fencing sheets had been wrenched away by the fierce winds that had been raging over the moorland for the last few days. A warning notice lay flat on the rough tussocky grass a few feet away from the shaft.

DANGER   DO NOT ENTER   DISUSED MINE

Then the voice came again.

"Who's there?" Jo asked nervously.

There was no reply—only the distant bleating of a sheep and the wailing of the gusty wind among the tin sheeting.

"Jo." Faintly she heard the call again.

"Who is it?"

"Come on, Jo!" This time the words were very distinct.

Jo hesitated. Hadn't she been warned about this old mine? Wasn't everyone supposed to keep clear of it? Suppose someone was in trouble, though, someone she could help. Besides, wasn't there something familiar about the voice?

She walked through the gap.

Below her, the shaft yawned—dim, desolate, and overgrown with brambles. Wooden boards that had originally covered the abyss hung in rotten shards. Looking down, Jo could see only darkness. Then, as her eyes became accustomed, she could make out gray rock and a ledge that sloped gently upward.

This was the place where they had brought them out, her memory told her. Uncle Jack, cousin Jem, and her father's mate Billy.

All killed in the pit disaster before Jo had been born. She had often cycled up here, curious about the dead men. Of course she'd seen photographs, but what had they *really* been like?

"Jo. What are you doing, lass? What's keeping you?"

Jo stared down into the void and the familiar memory stirred in her mind. "They never found your grandad, Jo, however much they dug." That's why she came up here really, to be with the grandfather she had never known.

"Come on, Jo. What's keeping you?"

"But who are you?"

"Some of my mates are trapped. Can you get down?" The voice was urgent now. "I've been trying to find a way out—a way out for us all. You've got to help me." The urgency increased.

"The way out's up here," said Jo desperately.

"I can't see anything—none of us can."

"I'll get help."

"No time. You coming, Jo?"

An instinct drove her on as she slithered down to the ledge, knowing what she was doing was crazy but unable to stop herself.

Still she couldn't see anything—just a black pit with what looked like sheer sides. She called down into it.

"Hello."

There was no reply.

"Hey!"

Still no reply.

"Where are you?"

The silence was like a wall. Then Jo felt the rock crumbling beneath her feet, breaking up. She pitched into the darkness.

Her shoulder hit something hard and the painful vibration echoed right through her body. Jo lay there shaking, not daring to move in case she plummeted further down, closing her eyes against the horror of it all, curling herself up into a womblike shape, cursing her own stupidity. Obviously she had imagined the voice. She *must* have done. Then, in her mounting fear, she hoped she hadn't, hoped against hope that there was someone there to help her.

"Where are you?" she whispered, then shouted.

Still no reply.

Jo shifted, reached out a hand, and froze as grim reality swept over her. She was on another ledge—this time narrower—and the void again stretched below in seemingly endless depth. Her shoulder hurt and she groaned with pain. Then, deep in the shaft below, Jo heard answering groans. So she wasn't on her own! Involuntarily, she moved backward—and encountered solid, warm, human flesh. Jo screamed again and again. "What's happening? What's happening?"

"You've got to help me, lass."

They were lying side by side—Jo and whoever it was. She could smell sweat mingled with coal dust.

"I got up here—trying to find a way out. The others are down below. Dying, most of them. But some might live—if we can help them." He gasped slightly.

"Are you hurt?"

"Can't breathe—not that well. But I'll be all right."

The groaning below continued, and then someone began to pray in a high, keening voice.

"There's a way out," said Jo. "Up there."

"I can't see anything. Must be dust in the eyes."

Jo turned to him at last, summoning up all her courage, but all she could see was a dark shape, half-buried under an overhanging lip of rock.

"I can see the light," she said. "I think we could climb there." She stared up at the pale sky which seemed a very long way above her.

"You'll have to help me."

"Okay." Trembling, Jo clambered to her feet, her shoulder pounding with pain.

"Can you stand?" she asked her companion.

"I don't know."

"Try."

Jo searched for, and found, a gnarled hand. She pulled and felt an answering weight. It dragged at her at first and then seemed not to be there.

"Where are you?"

"Here, lass." A gaunt shape was standing silently beside her and suddenly Jo felt the deathly chill of the wrist inside her fingers. She dropped it with a cry, the chill becoming ice, burning into her flesh. "Can't see nothing." The voice was distant now, almost like a sigh in the darkness, and Jo began to shake, the coldness spreading inside her so that she could hardly bear the pain. "Can't see a thing."

"The light's up there."

"I'll take your word for it. Show me where to climb."

"It's steep. I don't know if we'll manage it."

The drifting voice became sharper. "Look lively, lass, there's dying men down there."

"Give me your hand again."

For a moment she felt cobweb fingers. Then they passed through her own.

"Anyone down there?" The voice broke into the emptiness with unexpected harshness.

There was a face above her; a man with a helmet.

"Who are you?" Jo croaked, as if she hadn't spoken for a very long time. She was still shuddering all over and there was cold sweat on her forehead.

"Police. We were told the workings were open so we came up. Then I saw a bike and no one around. Are you hurt?"

"My shoulder, but it's not too bad. There are other people down here."

"Other people? How many?"

"I don't know. There's been a cave-in."

"What?"

"They're saying prayers. And there's a man beside me."

"Is there?" Her rescuer's voice was reassuring and sympathetic as the powerful beam of his flashlight swept the ledge. "I can't see anyone."

Jo turned quickly back to her companion. There was no one there, but she could make out something lying in the shadows. She leaned down and picked it up while the flashlight beam again doused the rock in brilliant white light. It was a miner's helmet, dented a little on its dome just above the flashlight, the way it was in the photograph. She stared at it.

"Hang on," said the policeman. "My partner's coming with a rope—and I'm going to lower him down to you. We'll have you up in no time."

"What about the others?"

"We'll get to them," the policeman replied in the same quiet, calm voice.

"Where are you?" called Jo.

There was no reply.

"*Who* are you?"

Still no reply.

A few seconds later, another policeman came down to her on a rope.

"I'm just going to slip this harness around your waist," he began.

"Wait."

"No time for that, lass." There was an edge to his voice and a certain unsteadiness. "There could be another rockfall any moment."

"What's that under the rock?"

He swept the dark cavity with his flashlight. "Could be a skeleton," he said uncertainly. "Yes...yes, I think it is. We'll look into that later." The policeman gulped, clearly wanting to get away as quickly as possible. "Come on!"

As Jo was swung up in the harness, she cradled the miner's helmet in her arms.

"This was my grandad's," she said to herself. "And now it's mine."

A LOATHLY LADY
Susan Price

A long, long time ago and a while before that, there were three brothers. And the eldest of these three brothers, he upped and said to his father, "I'm off to seek my fortune." And away he went, riding on a good horse, with a good greyhound running behind, and a good hawk on his wrist. And neither he, nor his horse, nor his greyhound, nor his hawk were ever seen again.

Now the second brother saddled his horse, took his hawk on his wrist, whistled for his greyhound, and rode off to search for the first brother, and maybe to find a fortune of his own. But he never came back either.

Now there was only the youngest brother left and, when he heard nothing from his two brothers, he upped and saddled his horse, took his hawk on his wrist, called his greyhound, and rode off to search for them.

He rode by hill, he rode by dale, and everyone he passed he asked for news of his brothers. Yes, they said, two young men had ridden this way before him—and so he kicked his horse and rode all the faster. Soon he was lost in a forest and didn't know how to go forward or back. But then he saw a hall through the trees and thought himself lucky. "Somewhere to shelter for the night," he said to his horse and his hound.

The hall was built of logs and roofed with shingles, but the shutters were hanging off, and the worm had got into the wood. No one had lived there for many years, and no one was around

54

now. The youngest brother tethered his horse outside the hall, rubbed her down, threw his cloak over her, and left her to graze. Inside the hall, his hawk flew into the rafters to perch, and he built himself a fire and settled down beside it with his hound.

As the hours passed, the dark grew close about the little fire, and the cold drafts grew sharper. The loose shutters banged in the wind, and the trees outside could be heard lashing themselves with their branches. The wind blew in around the broken door, making the fire flicker and scattering the old, dried rushes about the floor. And then came a sound like heavy tramping—a thumping of big, heavy feet—coming out of the forest, tramp, thump, closer and closer to the hall where the man and dog lay huddled together.

Thump! Tramp! Suddenly the doorway was filled by a dark shape. It ducked its head and into the firelight came a giantess, a hag, a monster—the ugliest old harridan you ever saw.

How can I tell you about her? Her hair was gray and hung down in greasy strings, so greasy it seemed her hair was soaking wet; and her skin was as greasy and gray as her hair. Red with blood her eyes were, with crusts of yellow matter at the corners, and the lower lids sagged to show wet, red linings. And so crossed were her eyes that she could only see the swollen end of her puffy red nose—from which ropes of thick, yellow snot hung to her chest. Her lips wouldn't close over her three yellow teeth, and she drooled.

Her spine was curved as much as a bent bow, and her big-knuckled, broken-nailed hands hung down by her bandy knees. The horny yellow nails on her toes were hard and sharp as flint and cut pieces out of the floor as she crossed it. And the smell of her! The smell that rolled off her as she came! The smell would choke a fox; it would curdle a cesspool; it would make a stone crumble.

This loathly lady came to the fireside, and she looked at the youngest brother and she said, "Food; give me food."

The reek of her, as she came close, made even the fire shrink back. Strings of snot and drool hung from her face and tangled in her greasy hair. But her eyes, though they were red and sore, were so sad as she looked at him, as if she knew too well her own ugliness. The young man was afraid, but

he could not bring himself to say anything that would make her eyes sadder. "If I had food, lady," he said, "I would share it with you gladly. But I have no food with me—I had hoped to be out of this forest before night."

The greyhound at his side was curling its lips at the hag, and growling. She looked down at it. "Food," she said.

"My good dog, lady."

"Meat," she said.

And her eyes were so sad, and her ugliness so gaunt, that it hurt the young man to refuse her the only food there was in the hall—yet it hurt him, too, to think of his good dog, which had loved and trusted him so long, being gobbled by that drooling mouth.

"Food," said the loathly lady, and whimpered. "Food," she said, and tears ran from her sore, sad, blood-red eyes.

"Take him, then," said the young man, and scrambled up from his place beside the fire and turned his back. Behind him he heard his dog snarl, and then shriek; and then a sound of breaking and gobbling, of tearing and gulping. And the young man put his hands to his face to catch the hot tears that spilled for his poor dog—and he could not tell if he did right to feed one poor hungry creature by ending the life of another.

Then the loathly lady spoke again. "More meat," she said.

The young man turned to find her looking up into the rafters, at his hawk which perched there. "My pretty hawk—she will only be a mouthful to you."

"More meat," said the loathly lady, and stared at him through hair and snot and grime with sad, sad red eyes.

With tears running down his own face, the young man raised his wrist and whistled, and the hawk flew down to him, fanning his face with air from her wings. She had hardly alighted before the lady snatched her away and crammed her whole into her mouth. The young man closed his eyes and turned away, and in a moment the hawk was eaten, bones and feathers and guts and all.

"More meat, more meat," said the loathly lady.

"There is only my poor horse."

"More meat," she said. So the young man went out into the night, untethered his horse, and led her back into the hall. He turned his face to the wall while the lady ate her, skin and bones

and hair and guts and all.

And if she asks for more meat, and there is only myself, he thought, how can I refuse her when I gave her my dog, my hawk and my horse?

But the next thing the lady said was, "A bed. A bed." Her tears splashed holes in the dirt floor. "Let me lie down and rest these long tired bones. Make me a bed."

The young man went out again and used his sword to cut soft green ferns. He carried them back in armfuls and made with them a deep bed, over which he spread his cloak, now that his horse needed it no longer. "Your bed, lady."

She lay down on the bed, and sighed, so glad was she to rest at last. "Now come and kiss me," she said.

To kiss that face besmeared with snot and drool, to have his own face besmeared by the grease of that rank hair—it made the young man tremble. But the sad, sad eyes stared at him, and he felt great pity for her. So he kissed her cheek—and fell senseless, stunned by her stink.

He woke when the sun shone in through the broken shutter and around the ill-fitting door. When he turned his head, he saw sleeping beside him the most beautiful girl that his eyes, or mine, or yours, had ever seen. Her hair spread over her shoulders, red-gold, shining. Her face was smooth and lovely, and her eyes a clear blue. She smiled, and she had all her teeth, and they were small and white.

She kissed him and said, "You gave me your dog, you gave me your hawk, you gave me your horse. And still more, you made me a bed and covered it with your cloak. But more still, you gave me a kiss, all to please me, ugly and frightening as I was. And now I give you myself, and my land, for I know your heart is gentle and your eyes see more than is before them. You will make a fine king."

And he looked about and saw a hall that was no longer a ruin, and was filled with rich things and comforts. And it would be easy to say that he made a fine king, and lived happily ever after with his beautiful queen.

But when he saw her smile, he remembered the hag's teeth crunching on the bones of his good dog, his hawk, his horse. And whatever became of his two brothers, who had ridden into the forest before him?

The beauty was a hag, and the hag was a beauty, and knowing that doesn't let you sleep peacefully at night.

THE GHOST ON SATURDAY NIGHT

Sid Fleischman

All over town signs had been tacked up:

THE GHOST IS COMING!

See the ghost of Crookneck John!

Famous Outlaw
Murderer
Bank Robber
Thief & Scoundrel.
Hung three times before he croaked!

⭐

THE GENUINE GHOST
Brought back to life by Professor Pepper,
the famous ghostraiser.
Don't miss this event.

Startling! Educational! Ladies welcome.

Saturday night, 8 p.m. sharp. Miners' Union Hall.
50 cents Admission

Everyone at school was talking about the ghost of Crookneck John. Talking about sneaking in, mostly. The trouble was there was no way to sneak into the Miners' Union Hall. It stood over the bank. The only way to get up there was by climbing a stairway along the side of the building. I was one of the lucky ones though. Aunt Etta and I had tickets.

Saturday morning arrived at last.

Then it was Saturday afternoon.

Then it was Saturday night.

Aunt Etta put on her hat and we set out for the Miners' Union Hall.

The hall was long and shadowy. Two oil lamps burned and smoked in front of the curtain. That's all the light there was.

We took chairs near the front and waited. Before long all the chairs were taken. And folks were standing along the walls.

"It's past eight o'clock," Aunt Etta announced.

We could hear noises behind the curtain. There were creaking sounds. And sawing sounds. And hammering sounds.

"Maybe it's the ghost," I said.

Aunt Etta shook her head. "Crookneck John was an outlaw—not a carpenter."

We waited. And waited some more.

At ten minutes to nine Professor Pepper stepped through the curtains.

"I will ask the ladies not to scream out," he announced in a deep voice.

"Moonshine," Aunt Etta whispered.

Professor Pepper took a grip on the lapel of his black frock coat. "What you will see tonight is stranger than strange. Odder than odd. Aye, a man deader than dead will walk among you. A

cutthroat, he was. Bank robber. The most feared outlaw of the century!"

I began to scrunch down in my chair. I couldn't help it.

"Hung once, he was," Professor Pepper went on. "Hung twice, he was. Hung three times before the meanness was jerked out of him! Aye, that's how he came to be known as Crookneck John."

"I don't wonder," Aunt Etta muttered. "Opie, sit up straight."

"Now then, I must have absolute silence!" Professor Pepper clapped his hands sharply.

The curtains parted.

A pine coffin was stretched across two sawhorses. It looked old and rotted, as if it had been dug out of the ground.

"Aye, the very box holding the bones of Crookneck John," the professor declared. "The coffin is six feet long. Crookneck John was almost seven feet. Buried with his knees bent up, he was. Most uncomfortable even for a ghost."

Then Professor Pepper clapped his hands again. His assistant, a toad-faced man, appeared and blew out the two oil lamps.

Pitch darkness closed in on the hall.

For a moment, I don't think anyone took a breath.

Professor Pepper's voice came rolling through the blackness.

"Crookneck John," he called. "I have your bones. Is the spirit willing to come forth, eh? Give a sign."

Silence. All I could hear was my own heart beating. Then there came a hollow rap-rap-rapping from the pine box.

"Aye, I hear the knock of your big knuckles, Mr. Crookneck John. Now rise up. Rise up your bloody bones and stretch your legs, sir."

My eyes strained to see through the darkness.

A minute went by. Maybe two or three. When Professor Pepper spoke again he was getting impatient.

"Rise up, you scoundrel! Ashamed to show your crooked neck to these honest folks, eh? This is Professor Pepper himself speaking. Aye, and I won't be made a fool of, sir!"

Black seconds ticked away. Then a minute or two. Professor Pepper became as short-tempered as a teased snake.

"Rise up, I say!" he commanded. "I've a hanging rope in my hand! Aye, and I'll string you up a *fourth* time!"

Silence.

And then there came a creaking of wood. And a groaning of nails. My neck went cold and prickly. *The lid of that pine coffin was lifting!*

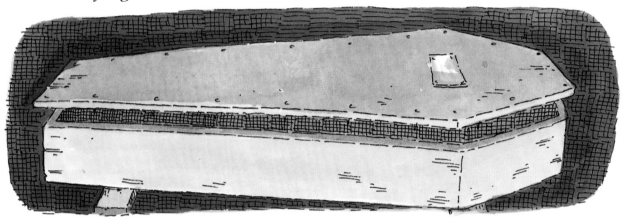

"That's better, you murdering scum!" snarled Professor Pepper.

It was scary to hear him talk that way to a dangerous outlaw about to rise from his coffin.

"I can't make out a thing," Aunt Etta said.

I stared hard, wanting to see that seven-foot ghost stretch his legs.

But suddenly the snarl went out of Professor Pepper's voice. "No! No!" he gasped. "Down! Back, sir! Not the rope!" Gurgling sounds escaped from his throat. "Help! Help! The lamps! Light the la—!"

I was sitting so straight by then I must have shot up six inches taller. The toad-faced man struck a match to the nearest lamp.

The air lit up. And there, against the curtain, staggered Professor Pepper. A hangman's noose was pulled tight around his neck.

The lid of the coffin stood open.

Professor Pepper clawed at the rope around his throat and caught a breath. "Save yourselves!" he croaked. "Run for your lives! Lock your doors! Shut your windows! Stay off the streets! The Crookneck Ghost is loose!"

The hall emptied in a whirlwind hurry. Even the toad-faced man was gone.

There was no one left but Professor Pepper, Aunt Etta, and me.

"Madam," he said. "I've been near strangled. Aye, short of breath I am. Perhaps that fine lad will help me carry the pine box downstairs."

I wasn't anxious to get *that* close to either Professor Pepper or the coffin.

"What on earth for?" Aunt Etta said.

"Why, Crookneck John must return to his dry bones before

the crow of dawn, madam. That's the way of ghosts, you know. I'll have the burying box moved to the jailhouse. He'll wake up behind bars, the scoundrel!"

Then he turned an eye on me. "I'll reward you for your trouble, lad. Cash money."

"Yes, sir," I answered.

"I've seen enough playacting for one night," Aunt Etta said. "It's past my bedtime. I'm going home, Opie."

"I won't be long," I said.

That pine box was heavy. I didn't think dry old bones could weigh so much. Then I reminded myself that Crookneck John had been seven feet tall.

The moon was rising and full.

When we struggled down to the foot of the stairs Professor Pepper's breath gave out.

"This'll do, lad," he said. "Oh, I should have known better than to raise the Crookneck Ghost on a full moon night. Turns him wild."

Then he dug in his coat pocket and handed me a coin. A mighty small one.

"Run home fast as you can, hear? Make sure that fine lady of yours is safe. I'll manage for myself."

"Much obliged for the cash money," I said politely. But I could tell from the feel that it was only a cent piece.

I didn't run home. I wasn't worried about Aunt Etta. She'd said it was all playacting. Professor Pepper *himself* could have done the rap-rap-rapping on the coffin. And he could have tied the noose around his *own* neck.

I wasn't even past the hotel when the moon faded out of the sky. The fog was creeping back.

I gave the cent piece a flip in the air and caught it. I put it in my pocket and then took it out again. Awfully clean and shiny, I thought, as if it had never been in use. Like Aunt Etta's rare Indian head penny in the bank safe.

There was just enough moonlight left to make out the date.

My breath caught. It was an 1877 Indian head penny. It appeared to be Aunt Etta's rare penny that she kept in the bank vault. But how had it come to be in Professor Pepper's pocket?

Just then I heard the snort of a horse and the creaking of wagon wheels.

"Bah! This fog's so thick I couldn't find my nose with both hands and a lantern."

I knew that voice. It belonged to Professor Pepper's assistant.

"I'm not interested in your nose, idiot!" It was the snarl of Professor Pepper himself. "Find the road. And quick before this town has the law on us."

The law? Suddenly I knew the only way Aunt Etta's rare penny could have got into the professor's pocket.

He'd robbed the bank!

69

"Give me those fool reins," he growled.

I had to do something. I felt my way along the hotel hitching post until I could make out the faint glow of their wagon lamp.

"Stop, sir!" I called out. "You're heading straight into a tree. Need help?"

"Help indeed!" said Professor Pepper. "Where's the road out of town, eh?"

Then he paused.

"Don't I know that voice?"

I was having a time to keep my teeth from clacking now. "Yes, sir," I said. "I'm Opie. I helped you down the stairs with the coffin."

"Well, take that nag by the nose and lead us out of here. When Crookneck John wakes up in the jailhouse he'll be after my blood."

More playacting, I thought! Oh, he was full of tricks. He'd scared folks into staying off the streets while he got away. But he hadn't counted on the fog.

Or me. An idea had already sprung into my head.

I led the horse and wagon step by step along the road toward home. When I came to the dip, I stopped. We were at one end of the old Horseshoe Mine.

"There's a big tunnel on the left, sir. About two miles long. It's kind of a short cut through the fog."

"Aye, a short cut would please me!" the professor laughed.

A moment later they went clattering into the mine tunnel.

I was in such a hurry to reach Mr. Whitman's house that I must have banged my shins six times and run into a wall at least once.

Mr. Whitman owned the bank. I showed him Aunt Etta's 1877 one-cent piece. I told him I thought Professor Pepper had robbed the safe. And we went for the sheriff.

Sure enough, the bank safe was empty.

"But the walls of the bank are solid stone," Mr. Whitman said. "How did he get in?"

I had already noticed bits of sawdust. I looked up. The sheriff looked up.

"Yup," he said. "Professor Pepper cut through the floor of the Miners' Union Hall upstairs. Probably let himself down with the hangman's rope and up again. Then hammered the wood back in place."

I remembered hearing hammer sounds behind the curtain during the long wait for the show to start.

"And he must have hoped we'd believe it was the Crookneck Ghost who'd robbed the bank," the sheriff said. "Well, Professor Pepper can't have got far in this fog."

"Not far at all," I said. "He's in the Horseshoe Mine."

"The Horseshoe Mine!" the sheriff said.

"Yes, sir."

"Doesn't he know it makes a perfect horseshoe and comes out about forty feet from the jailhouse?"

"No, sir," I smiled. "I didn't tell him that."

So the sheriff waited at the end of the tunnel. His three deputies waited. And I waited, too.

Before long we could hear the echo of horse's hooves. My heart began to beat a little faster. The glow of a lantern appeared like a firefly deep in the tunnel.

The sheriff lifted his shotgun and nodded to his deputies. "Get ready, boys. The rest of you stay back."

The wagon lantern grew larger and brighter. Then I could see Professor Pepper himself—chuckling and singing.

But when he saw the law waiting for him he gave a gasp and a groan.

"Great jumping hop toads!" he cried out. He grabbed the reins and tried to turn the wagon around. But the mine shaft wasn't wide enough. He kept snapping the whip, but all the horse could do was snort and whinny.

The sheriff charged forward and caught the horse by the halter.

"That will do, gents," he said. "Welcome back to Golden Hill. Easy, now, or you'll end up buckshot ghosts."

"Thunder and lightning," the professor snarled. "We've been outfoxed!"

The deputies led him away, together with his toad-faced assistant.

The sheriff climbed on the wagon and called to me.

"Opie. Did you say this coffin was uncommon heavy?"

"Yes, sir."

"Hold the lantern."

As I held the lantern, he pried off the lid. There were no bones in that pine box at all.

It was full of money. The stolen bank money.

"Opie," said the sheriff, "I think you're due for a reward..."

SIREN SONG
Vivien Alcock

1st August 1981

Dear Tape Recorder,

This is me. My name's Roger and I'm nine years old today. You're my birthday present.

> Happy birthday to me,
> Happy birthday to you,
> Happy birthday, dear both-of-us...

1st August 1982

R for Roger. R for Roger. This is Roger, mark ten, calling. I'm not going to bore you with a bite-by-bite account of my birthday party, like last year. This time I'll only record the exciting moments of my life. Over and out.

1st August 1983

My name is Roger Kent. I am eleven years old. I want to get this down in case anything happens to me.

I hate this town. I wish we hadn't come to live here. There's something funny about it.

For one thing, there are no other children here. Except Billy Watson, and he's weird. He's a thin, white-faced boy who jumps when you speak to him. Mom says he's been ill, and I must be kind. I was. I asked him to

74

come to my birthday party today. He twitched like I'd stabbed him in the back, and his eyes scuttled about like beetles. Then he mumbled something and ran off.

The grown-ups are peculiar, too. They're old and baggy-eyed, as if they'd been crying all night. When they see me, they stop talking. They watch me. It's a bit scary.

At first I thought they didn't like me. But it's not that. They look as if they know something terrible's going to happen to me, and are sorry about it.

Mrs. Mason's the worst. I hate the way she looks at me. Her eyes are...I dunno...sort of hungry. I don't mean she's a cannibal. It's more like...d'you know why gerbils sometimes eat their own babies? It's because they're afraid they're in danger, and think they'll be safer inside.

That's just how Mrs. Mason looks at me. As if she'd like to swallow me to keep me safe. But what from?

This morning, when she heard it was my birthday, she hugged me. I jerked away. I didn't mean to be rude. I honestly thought she was going to start nibbling my ear. That's the sort of state I'm in.

"Never go out at night," she said. (That's nothing. Mom's always telling me that nowadays. It's what came next.) "Never go out at night, *whatever sounds you hear!*"

Funny thing to say, wasn't it? "Whatever sounds you hear."

I've been thinking and thinking, but I can't imagine what she meant. If we lived by the sea, I'd think of smugglers. You know, like that poem—"Watch the wall, my darling, while the gentlemen go by."

Perhaps they're witches! I'm not being silly. There *are* witches nowadays. It was in the papers once. COVEN OF WITCHES EXPOSED, it said. They certainly were exposed! There was this photograph of men and women with nothing on. Not that you could see much, only their backs. They didn't look wild and exciting at all. Just stupid. And cold—you could almost see the goose pimples. Still, they were witches.

D'you think it's that?

Full moon tonight. I'm going to stay awake and listen. It must be happening somewhere near enough for me to hear, or she wouldn't have said that.

Supposing they use our backyard?

Suppose Mom's joined them! She's been a bit strange lately. No, that's silly.

10:30 P.M. I'm sitting by the window. Nothing's happened yet. Just the usual night noises, and not many of those. This town dies after ten o'clock. A dog barking. An owl getting on my nerves, can't the stupid thing say anything else?

It's boring. I think I'll go to bed for a bit.

Midnight. I've got a digital clock and it says: 00:00. Like Time's laid eggs in a row. No time. Nothing point nothing, nothing time. Don't count your minutes before they're hatched.

What's that?

Only an owl. The window's wide open, and it's cold. The moon is round and bright. There are shadows all over the yard. I can't see anything. It's very quiet now. No wind.

Listen!

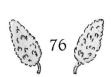

Children! I can hear children laughing. I can hear their voices calling softly . . .

I think they're in Billy Watson's yard. He must be having a midnight party, and he hasn't asked me! Pig! No wonder he ran off when I invited him to my party.

I wish I could see them. There're too many trees. Too many shadows.

Listen!

This microphone's too small. I held it out of the window, but I didn't get anything. They were singing. Their voices were high and clear. I could hear every word. It was a funny little tune. Sort of sad, but nice. There's a chorus where they all hoot softly like baby owls. I think I can remember the words —

> Little ghost, all dressed in white,
> Walking on a summer's night,
> (Hoooo, hooo,)
> Calling to her childhood friend,
> Asking him to come and play,
> But his hair stands up on end.
> Billy Watson runs away.

Billy Watson! So they are friends of his! I suppose they're playing a game . . .

Listen . . .

It was a girl singing alone this time. I'm sure it was a girl. Her voice was so high and sweet and sad, it made me ache. This is what she sang —

Don't you love me any more?
I'm as pretty as before.
(Hooo, hooo,)
Though my roses are all gone,
Lily-white is just as sweet.
Stars shine through me now, not on
Flesh that's only so much meat.

I wish I could see her . . .

"Yoo-hoo! Over here!"

They heard me. I know they did. They're whispering. Now they're coming nearer. I can hear the bushes rustling by our wall. Look! I think one of them's slipped into our yard. It's difficult to be sure. There are so many shadows. I'm going to dangle the microphone out of the window . . .

Listen!

Billy, see the moon is bright.
Won't you play with me tonight?
(Hooo, hooo,)
Billy Watson's now in bed,
With his fingers in his ears,
And his blankets hide his head,
And his face is wet with tears.

I got it that time! It's very faint, but you can just make out the words. I don't think they can be friends of Billy's after all. They sounded as if they were mocking him. I wonder who they are?

Oh, they're going away now! I can hear them running through the bushes, laughing. They're gone!

No. There's still one standing in the shadow of the lilac tree. Just below my window. I'm sure it's the girl. I can see her white dress gleaming...unless it's just moonlight. She's all alone now. Waiting for me.

Listen!

> Little ghost all dressed in white
> Singing sadly in the night,
> (Hooo, hooo,)
> Who will play with me instead?
> Must I be lonely till the end?
> Is there any child abed
> Brave enough to be my friend?

I'm coming! Wait for me! I know I promised Mom I'd never go out at night, but...the moon is shining bright as day. Someone is singing in the yard below. Softly. Sweetly. Surely it won't matter if I go out just once?

The rest of the tape is blank. Roger Kent was never seen again.